Adventures of COW TOO

by
COW

as told to Lori Korchek

and photographed by Marshall Taylor

TRICYCLE PRESS
Berkeley • Toronto

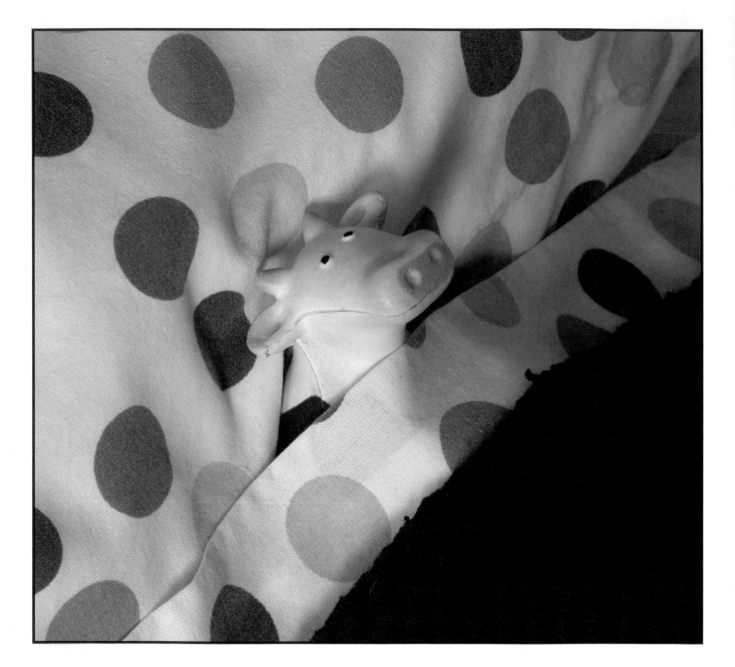

One day Cow woke up to an exciting new adventure.

"I've chipped my nose. Will you go to the grocery store for me?"
Cow's mom asked.

Cow jumped for joy.

Cow took a train to the store.

"Here we go!"

First stop, green beans.

"Yum, bananas."

"Now, where are those oranges?"

"Here they are!"

Cow looked for the very best apples so Ma could bake a pie.

"Gosh, these grapes are heavy."

"Excuse me, ladies, where would I find the mayonnaise?"

Cow wondered what a frog was doing on a jar of mayo.

Cow almost forgot the ice cream. "I'll get two."

Happy, Cow smiled and said, "Peeeeeeas!"

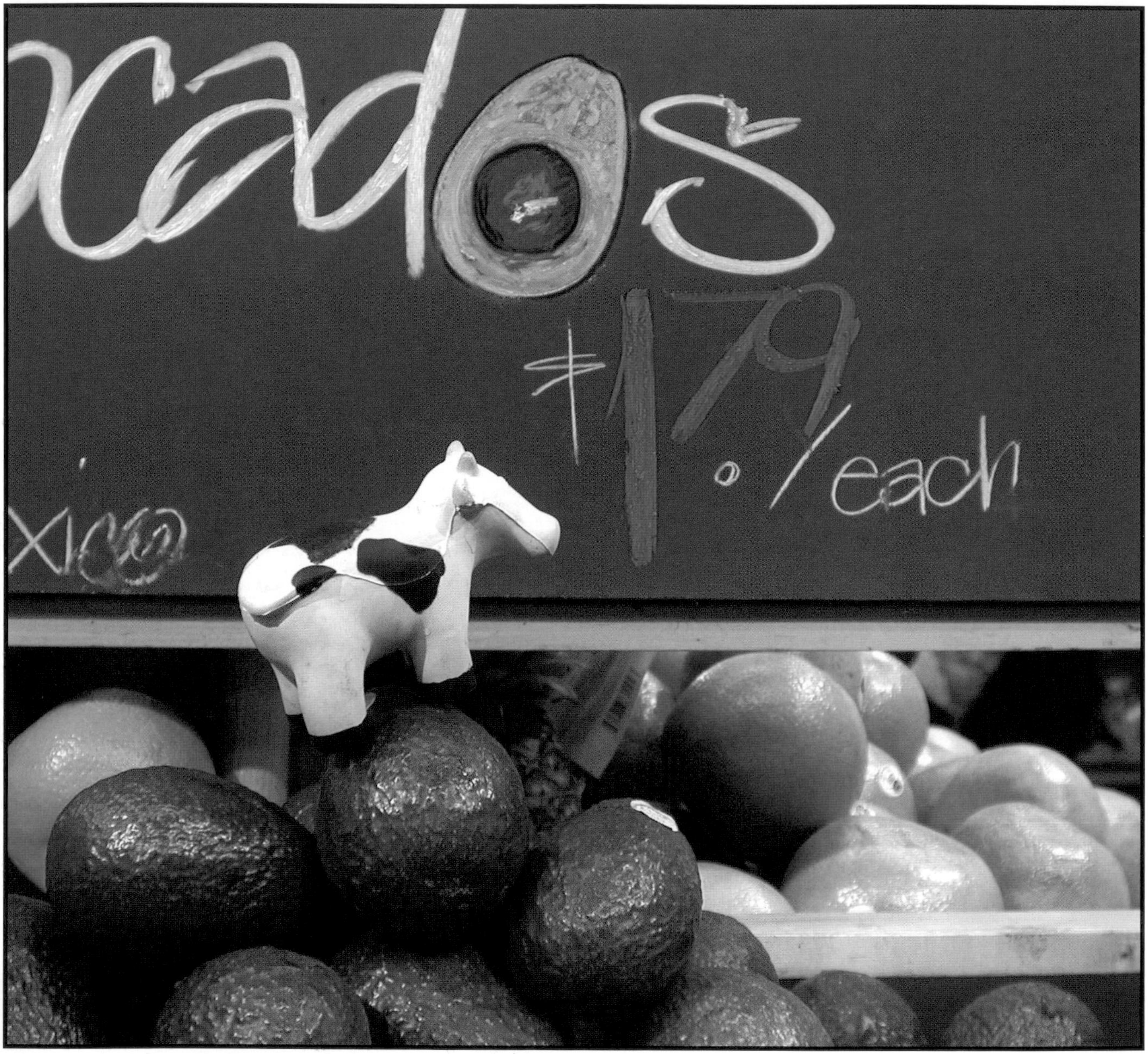
cados
$1.79/each
xico

The clock said 1:79. It was time to go!

"Paper or plastic?" asked the nice grocery lady.
"I'm plastic, thank you," said Cow.

Cow's dad was waiting at the door. "Hi, Pop!"

"Good job," said Aunt Ernie. "You deserve some ice cream."

But Cow just wanted to go to the movies.
So they did.

Tricycle Press
an imprint of Ten Speed Press
PO Box 7123
Berkeley, California 94707
www.tricyclepress.com

Cow logo and milk carton packaging are registered trade-
marks of Farmland Dairies LLC. All marks are used with
the kind permission of Farmland Dairies LLC.

Design by Betsy Stromberg
Typeset in Clarendon

Library of Congress Cataloging-in-Publication Data

Korchek, Lori, 1959-
  Adventures of Cow, too / by Cow as told to Lori
Korchek ; photographed by Marshall Taylor.
      p. cm.
  Summary: A very excited toy cow takes an adventurous
trip to a grocery store.
  ISBN-13: 978-1-58246-189-2
  ISBN-10: 1-58246-189-9
[1. Grocery shopping—Fiction. 2. Toys—Fiction.
3. Cows—Fiction. 4. Humorous stories.] I. Taylor,
Marshall, 1957- ill. II. Title.
  PZ7.K83637Adt 2006
  [E]--dc22
                                        2006006839

First Tricycle Press printing, 2007
Printed in China

1 2 3 4 5 6 — 11 10 09 08 07